Strega Nona

an original tale written and illustrated
by Tomie dePaola

Aladdin Paperbacks

For Franny and Fuffy

Aladdin Paperbacks
An imprint of Simon & Schuster
Children's Publishing Division
1230 Avenue of the Americas
New York, NY 10020
Copyright © 1975 by Tomie dePaola
All rights reserved including the right of reproduction
in whole or in part in any form.
Also available in a hardcover edition from
Simon & Schuster Books for Young Readers

40 39 38 37 36

0-671-66606-1

Library of Congress Cataloging in Publication Data

de Paola, Thomas Anthony. Strega Nona.
SUMMARY: When Strega Nona leaves him alone with her magic
pasta pot, Big Anthony is determined to show the townspeople how
it works. [1. Folklore—Italy] I. Title. PZ8.1.D43St
[398.2'2'0945] [E] 75-11565

In a town in Calabria, a long time ago, there lived an old lady everyone called Strega Nona, which meant "Grandma Witch."

Although all the people in town talked about her in whispers, they all went to see her if they had troubles. Even the priest and the sisters of the convent went, because Strega Nona *did* have a magic touch.

She could cure a headache, with oil and water and a hairpin.

She made special potions for the girls who wanted husbands.

And she was very good at getting rid of warts.

But Strega Nona was getting old, and she needed someone to help her keep her little house and garden, so she put up a sign in the town square

And Big Anthony, who didn't pay attention, went to see her.

"Anthony," said Strega Nona, "you must sweep the house and wash the dishes. You must weed the garden and pick the vegetables. You must feed the goat and milk her. And you must fetch the water. For this, I will give you three coins and a place to sleep and food to eat."

"Oh, *grazie,*" said Big Anthony.

"The one thing you must never do," said Strega Nona, "is touch the pasta pot. It is very valuable and I don't let anyone touch it!"

"Oh, *si,* yes," said Big Anthony.

And so the days went by. Big Anthony did his work and Strega Nona met with the people who came to see her for headaches and husbands and warts.

Big Anthony had a nice bed to sleep in next to the goat shed, and he had food to eat.

One evening when Big Anthony was milking the goat, he heard Strega Nona singing. Peeking in the window, he saw Strega Nona standing over the pasta pot.

She sang,

> Bubble, bubble, pasta pot,
> Boil me some pasta, nice and hot,
> I'm hungry and it's time to sup,
> Boil enough pasta to fill me up.

And the pasta pot bubbled and boiled and was suddenly filled with steaming hot pasta.

Then Strega Nona sang,

> Enough, enough, pasta pot,
> I have my pasta, nice and hot,
> So simmer down my pot of clay,
> Until I'm hungry another day.

"How wonderful!" said Big Anthony. "That's a magic pot for sure!"

And Strega Nona called Big Anthony in for supper.

But too bad for Big Anthony, because he didn't see Strega Nona blow three kisses to the magic pasta pot.

And this is what happened.

The next day when Big Anthony went to the town square to fetch the water, he told everyone about the pasta pot.

And naturally everyone laughed at him, because it sounded so silly—a pot that cooked all by itself.

"You'd better go and confess to the priest, Big Anthony," they said. "Such a lie!"

And Big Anthony was angry and that wasn't a very good thing to be.

"I'll show them!" he said to himself. "Someday I will get the Pasta Pot and make it cook! And then *they'll* be sorry."

That day came sooner than even Big Anthony would have thought, because two days later Strega Nona said to Big Anthony, "Anthony, I must go over the mountain to the next town to see my friend, Strega Amelia. Sweep the house and weed the garden. Feed the goat and milk her and for your lunch, there are some bread and cheese in the cupboard. And remember, don't touch the pasta pot."

"Oh, yes—yes—Strega Nona," said Big Anthony. But inside he was thinking, *My chance has come!*

As soon as Strega Nona was out of sight, Big Anthony went inside, pulled the pasta pot off the shelf and put it on the floor.

"Now, let's see if I can remember the words," said Big Anthony.
And Big Anthony sang,

> Bubble, bubble, pasta pot,
> Boil me some pasta, nice and hot,
> I'm hungry and it's time to sup,
> Boil enough pasta to fill me up.

And sure enough, the pot bubbled and boiled and began to fill up with pasta.

"Aha!" said Big Anthony, and he ran to the town square, jumped on the fountain and shouted, "Everyone get forks and plates and platters and bowls. Pasta for all at Strega Nona's house. Big Anthony has made the magic pasta pot work."

Of course everyone laughed, but ran home to get forks and plates and platters and bowls, and sure enough, when they got to Strega Nona's the pasta pot was so full it was beginning to overflow.

Big Anthony was a hero!

He scooped out pasta and filled the plates and platters and bowls.

There was more than enough for all the townspeople, including the priest and the sisters from the convent.

And some people came back for two and three helpings, but the pot was never empty.

When all had had their fill, Big Anthony sang,
                    Enough, enough, my pasta pot,
                    I have my pasta nice and hot.
                    So simmer down, my pot of clay
                    Until I'm hungry another day.
But, alas, he did not blow the three kisses!

He went outside and to the applause of the crowd, Big Anthony took a bow.

He was so busy listening to compliments from everyone that he didn't notice the pasta pot was still bubbling and boiling, until a sister from the convent said, "Oh, Big Anthony, look!"

And pasta was pouring out of the pot all over the floor of Strega Nona's house and was coming out the door!

Big Anthony rushed in and shouted the magic words again, but the pot kept bubbling.

He took the pot off the floor, but pasta kept on pouring from it.

Big Anthony grabbed a cover and put it on the pot and sat on it.

But the pasta raised the cover, and Big Anthony as well, and spilled on the floor of Strega Nona's house.

"Stop!" yelled Big Anthony.

But the pasta did not stop and if someone hadn't grabbed poor Big Anthony, the pasta would have covered him up. The pasta had all but filled the little house.

Out of the windows and through the doors came the pasta and the pot kept right on bubbling.

The townspeople began to worry.

"Do something, Big Anthony," they shouted.

Big Anthony sang the magic song again but without the three kisses it did no good!

By this time the pasta was on its way down the road and all the people were running to keep ahead of it.

"We must protect our town from the pasta," shouted the mayor. "Get mattresses, tables, doors—anything to make a barricade."

But even that didn't work. The pot kept bubbling and the pasta kept coming!

"We are lost," said the people, and the priest and the sisters of the convent began praying. "The pasta will cover our town," they cried.

And it certainly would have, had Strega Nona not come down the road, home from her visit.

She didn't have to look twice to know what had happened.

She sang the magic song and blew the three kisses and with a sputter the pot stopped boiling and the pasta came to a halt.

"Oh, *grazia*—thank you, thank you, Strega Nona," the people cried.

But then they turned on poor Big Anthony.
"String him up," the men of the town shouted.

"Now, wait," said Strega Nona. "The punishment must fit the crime." And she took a fork from a lady standing nearby and held it out to Big Anthony.

"All right, Anthony, you wanted pasta from my magic pasta pot," Strega Nona said," and *I* want to sleep in my little bed tonight. So start eating."

And he did—poor Big Anthony.